Pettranella

By Betty Waterton
Illustrations by Ann Blades

A Meadow Mouse Paperback
Douglas & McIntyre
Toronto/Vancouver

Long ago in a country far away lived a little girl named Pettranella. She lived with her father and mother in the upstairs of her grandmother's tall, narrow house.

Other houses just like it lined the street on both sides, and at the end of the street was the mill. All day and all night smoke rose from its great smokestacks and lay like a grey blanket over the city. It hid the sun and choked the trees, and it withered the flowers that tried to grow in the window boxes.

One dark winter night when the wind blew cold from the east, Pettranella's father came home with a letter. The family gathered around the table in the warm yellow circle of the lamp to read it; even the grandmother came from her rooms downstairs to listen.

"It's from Uncle Gus in Canada," began her father. "He has his homestead there now, and is already clearing his land. Someday it will be a large farm growing many crops of grain." And then he read the letter aloud.

When he had finished, Pettranella said, "I wish we could go there, too, and live on a homestead."

Her parents looked at each other, their eyes twinkling with a secret. "We *are* going," said her mother. "We are sailing on the very next ship."

Pettranella could hardly believe her ears. Suddenly she thought of some things she had always wanted. "Can we have some chickens?" she asked. "And a swing?"

"You will be in charge of the chickens," laughed her father, "and I will put up a swing for you in our biggest tree."

"And Grandmother," cried Pettranella, "now you will have a real flower garden, not just a window box."

Pulling her close, the grandmother said gently, "But I cannot go to the new land with you, little one. I am too old to make such a long journey."

Pettranella's eyes filled with tears. "Then I won't go either," she said.

But in the end, of course, she did.

When they were ready to leave, her grandmother gave her a small muslin bag. Pettranella opened it and looked inside. "There are seeds in here!" she exclaimed.

"There is a garden in there," said the old lady. "Those are flower seeds to plant when you get to your new home."

"Oh, I will take such good care of them," promised Pettranella. "And I will plant them and make a beautiful garden for you."

So they left their homeland. It was sad, thought Pettranella, but it was exciting, too. Sad to say good-bye to everyone they knew, and exciting to be going across the ocean in a big ship.

But the winter storms were not over, and as the ship pitched about on the stormy seas everyone was seasick. For days Pettranella lay on her wooden bunk in the crowded hold, wishing she was back home in her clean, warm bed.

At last they reached the shores of Canada. Pettranella began to feel better. As they stood at the rail waiting to leave the ship, she asked, "Can we see our homestead yet?"

Not yet, they told her; there was still a long way to go.

Before they could continue their journey her father had to fill out many forms, and Pettranella spent hours and hours sitting on their round-topped trunk in a crowded building, waiting. So many people, she thought. Would there be room for them all?

Finally one day the last form was signed and they were free to go, and as they travelled up a wide river and across the lonely land, Pettranella knew that in this big country there would be room for everyone.

After many days they came to a settlement where two rivers met and there they camped while the father got his homestead papers. Then they bought some things they would need: an axe and a saw, a hammer and nails, sacks of food and seed, a plow and a cow and a strong brown ox, and a cart with two large wooden wheels. And some chickens.

The ox was hitched to the cart, which was so full of all their belongings that there was barely room for Pettranella and her mother. Her father walked beside the ox, and the cow followed.

The wooden wheels creaked over the bumpy ground, and at first Pettranella thought it was fun, but soon she began asking, "When are we going to get there?" and making rather a nuisance of herself climbing in and out of the cart.

Often at night as they lay wrapped in their warm quilts beside the fire, they heard owls hooting, and sometimes wolves calling to one another; once they saw the northern lights.

One day as they followed the winding trail through groves of spruce and poplar, there was a sudden THUMP, CRACK, CRASH!

"What happened?" cried Pettranella, as she slid off the cart into the mud.

"We have broken a shaft," said her father. "One of the wheels went over a big rock."

"Now we'll never find our homestead!" wailed Pettranella, as they began to unload the cart. "We'll make a new shaft," said her father; and, taking his axe, he went into the woods to cut a pole the right size.

Pettranella helped her mother make lunch, then sat down on a log to wait. Taking the bag of seeds from her pocket, she poured them out into a little pile on her lap, thinking all the while of the garden she would soon be making.

Just then she heard something. A familiar creaking and squeaking, and it was getting closer. It had to be — it was — another ox cart!

"Somebody's coming!" she shouted, jumping up.

Her father came running out of the woods as the cart drew near. It was just like theirs, but the ox was black. The driver had a tanned, friendly face. When he saw their trouble, he swung down from his cart to help.

He helped the father make a new shaft, then they fastened it in place and loaded the cart again.

Afterwards they all had lunch, and Pettranella sat listening while the grownups talked together. Their new friend had a homestead near theirs, he said, and he invited them to visit one day.

"Do you have any children?" asked Pettranella.

"A little girl just like you," he laughed, as he climbed into his cart. He was on his way to get some supplies. Pettranella waved good-bye as he drove off, and they set forth once again to find their homestead. "Our neighbour says it isn't far now," said her father.

As they bumped along the trail, suddenly Pettranella thought about the flower seeds. She felt in her pocket, but there was nothing there. The muslin bag was gone!

"Oh, oh! Stop!" she cried. "The seeds are gone!"

Her father halted the ox. "I saw you looking at them before lunch," said her mother. "You must have spilled them there. You'll never find them now."

"I'm going back to look anyway," said Pettranella, and, before they could stop her, she was running back down the trail.

She found the log, but she didn't find any seeds. Just the empty muslin bag.

As she trudged back to the cart, her tears began to fall. "I was going to make such a beautiful garden, and now I broke my promise to Grandmother!"

"Maybe you can make a vegetable garden instead," suggested her mother, but Pettranella knew it wouldn't be the same. "I don't think turnips and cabbages are very pretty," she sighed.

It was later that afternoon, near teatime, when they found their homestead.

Their own land, as far as they could see! Pettranella was so excited that for a while she forgot all about her lost seeds.

That night they slept on beds of spruce and tamarack boughs cut from their own trees. What a good smell, thought Pettranella, snuggling under her quilt.

The next morning her father began to put up a small cabin; later he would build a larger one. Then he started to break the land. A small piece of ground was set aside for vegetables, and after it was dug, it was Pettranella's job to rake the earth and gather the stones into a pile.

"Can we plant the seeds now?" she asked when she had finished.

"Not yet," said her mother, "it's still too cold."

One morning they were awakened by a great noise that filled the sky above them. "Wild geese!" shouted the father, as they rushed outside to look. "They're on their way north. It's really spring!"

Soon squirrels chattered and red-winged blackbirds sang, a wobbly-legged calf was born to the cow, and sixteen baby chicks hatched.

"Now we can plant the garden," said the mother, and they did.

Early the next morning Pettranella ran outside to see if anything had sprouted yet. The soil was bare; but a few days later when she looked, she saw rows of tiny green shoots.

If only I hadn't lost Grandmother's seeds, she thought, flowers would be coming up now, too.

One warm Sunday a few weeks later, Pettranella put on a clean pinafore and her best sunbonnet and went to help her father hitch up the ox, for this was the day they were going to visit their neighbours.

As the ox cart bumped and bounced down the trail over which they had come so many weeks before, Pettranella thought about the little girl they were going to visit. She will probably be my very best friend, she thought to herself.

Suddenly her father stopped the cart and jumped down. "There's the rock where we broke the shaft," he said. "This time I will lead the ox around it."

"There's where we had lunch that day," said her mother.

"And there's the log I was sitting on when I lost the seeds," said Pettranella. "And look! LOOK AT ALL THOSE FLOWERS!"

There they were. Blowing gently in the breeze, their bright faces turned to the sun and their roots firm in the Canadian soil — Grandmother's flowers.

"Oh! Oh!" cried Pettranella, "I have never seen such beautiful flowers!"

Her mother's eyes were shining as she looked at them. "Just like the ones that grew in the countryside back home!" she exclaimed.

"You can plant them beside our house," said her father, "and make a flower garden there."

Pettranella did, and she tended it carefully, and so her promise to her grandmother was not broken after all.

But she left some to grow beside the trail, that other settlers might see them and not feel lonely; and to this very day, Pettranella's flowers bloom each year beside a country road in Manitoba.

For Julie

A Meadow Mouse Paperback
Douglas & McIntyre Ltd.
585 Bloor Street West
Toronto, Ontario M6G 1K5

Third paperback edition 1991
Printed and bound in Hong Kong
by Everbest Printing Co., Ltd.

Canadian Cataloguing in Publication Data

Waterton, Betty
    Pettranella

ISBN 0-88899-108-8

I. Blades, Ann. II. Title.

PS8595.A796P48 1989   jC813'.54   C90-093072-1
PZ7.W37Pe 1989